48 Hours W

Mij Kelly

PUFFIN BOOKS

PUFFIN BOOKS

Published by the Penguin Group
Penguin Books Ltd, 27 Wrights Lane, London W8 5TZ, England
Penguin Books USA Inc., 375 Hudson Street, New York, New York 10014, USA
Penguin Books Australia Ltd, Ringwood, Victoria, Australia
Penguin Books Canada Ltd, 10 Alcorn Avenue, Toronto, Ontario, Canada M4V 3B2
Penguin Books (NZ) Ltd, 182–190 Wairau Road, Auckland 10, New Zealand

Penguin Books Ltd, Registered Offices: Harmondsworth, Middlesex, England

First published by Blackie 1993
Published in Puffin Books 1995
1 3 5 7 9 10 8 6 4 2

Printed in England by Clays Ltd, St Ives plc

The first thing you should know about Joe and Gertie Stein is that they lived in an enormous dark house with cobwebs in the corners and bats in the roof space.

The second thing you should know is that they were both ordinary children with parents who made them eat sprouts and sent them to bed at the same time every night.

And the third thing you should know is that when you live in a house the size of a castle there's a world of difference between being sent to bed and actually going.

Night after night Mr and Mrs Stein would sit watching the television in the downstairs living-room, blissfully unaware that instead of drifting off to sleep in the third-floor bedroom, their children were running wild through the house.

Through ringing cellars, up narrow spiral staircases leading to high turrets, across vast attics, Gertie and Joe scampered, with knapsacks on their backs and torches in their hands.

And their parents knew nothing of it.

9.30 P.M. THURSDAY

'Why do my children always have bags under their eyes?' Mrs Stein asked one night. She folded her newspaper and looked inquiringly at her husband.

Mr Stein got up to adjust the television set.

'Perhaps they don't get enough sleep,' he said. 'We'll start sending them to bed half an hour earlier. This telly's playing up a bit. I think we're in for a storm.'

Meanwhile, upstairs in the third-floor bedroom, Gertie was stuffing a spare jumper into her knapsack and checking the batteries in her torch.

'Where shall we go tonight?' she asked.

Joe was looking out of the window. 'It's beginning to rain,' he said. 'That means the cellar will be flooded and the attics will be leaking.'

'Which leaves us the turrets, the west wing or the labs,' said Gertie.

'Not the labs,' said Joe. 'Not in the dark.'

Gertie and Joe's parents were research biologists, which meant that they spent a lot of time tinkering with test-tubes and squinting at computer screens. They both worked at home, so they had converted several rooms on the east side of the house into laboratories. They never kept anything *really* horrible in there, just a few gallons of blood on which they 'ran tests', but . . .

'Not the labs!' Joe repeated, in case Gertie hadn't got the message.

'It's only blood,' said Gertie tetchily. 'It can't throw itself out of the test-tube at you.' She thought a moment. 'I know, let's go to the west wing. We haven't been there for ages.' And she switched on her torch with a practised flick of her thumb.

10.15 P.M. THURSDAY

The west wing was full of clutter – room upon room, floor upon floor of junk.

'It's got worse,' said Joe, shining his torch into the first room. 'There's even more stuff here than last time.'

Rolls of carpet, discarded lampshades, torn umbrellas, dusty tea-chests, musty wardrobes, rusty kettles – anything useless or past it, the Steins kept. And if any of their friends were spring-cleaning and wanted to get rid of a broken sewing machine or a battered chest of drawers, the Steins would give it house room. 'Oh no,' they'd say, 'you can't chuck it out! If you get rid of it you're bound to need it again. Why not store it in our west wing?'

'These books weren't here last time,' said Gertie, starting to leaf through a pile of paperbacks, torch in hand, for all as if she had dropped into her local library. She was just getting involved in the adventures of twelve princesses and their dancing slippers when Joe interrupted her with a shout.

'Look what I found!'

Gertie jumped, and her torch clattered to the floor.

'This better be worth it,' she muttered, picking her way over to Joe. 'I think my bulb's broken.'

It was worth it. Neither Gertie nor Joe had ever had a doll. Their parents had simply never thought to buy them one. They had chemistry sets, microscopes and shelves of encyclopaedias, but never a teddy or a doll. And now they were both too old even to think of wanting one. But here, here was a doll you could never be too old for.

It was an old dummy from a shop window, a plastic mannequin with a black wig and a faded grey suit forty years out of date.

'How utterly brilliant,' breathed Gertie, reaching up to straighten the wig. 'I wonder where he came from . . .'

'Look, we can unscrew him at the waist. You take the legs and I'll take the rest of him.' Joe jammed his torch between his teeth and set to work. 'We can take him to the turret.'

There were four turrets, one at each corner of the house, and they were all exactly the same with long spiral staircases and a small circular room at the top. Well, three were the same and one was special, because Gertie and Joe had turned it into a den. They had raided the best rugs and cushions from the west wing and built themselves a wonderful hidey-hole for midnight feasts and early morning card games.

It was a great place to watch the sun rise. That's why they had picked it, but the unfortunate result was that it stood at the south-east corner of the house, on the far side of the laboratories.

Gertie sighed and gripped the dummy round the ankles.

It wasn't easy making their way right from one end of that enormous house to the other with a six-foot plastic mannequin and one torch between them. To make things worse, a storm was raging by the time they reached the labs. They could hear the wind buffeting the windows, and the distant roar of thunder.

'Can't we go the other way?' asked Joe.

'No, it would take far too long,' snapped Gertie, who was having difficulty manoeuvring the legs. She pushed open the door to the main laboratory and stepped inside. The plastic legs, which she had jammed under her arm, swung wildly.

There was a terrible crash and then silence.

After a minute or two, Joe started. 'You are the most clumsy person I've ever met,' he hissed out of the darkness above his torch. 'Why is it that whenever something can be dropped, you . . .'

'Shut up!' whispered Gertie, her courage returning. 'Here, give me your torch. I want to see if I've broken anything.'

'Why don't you just switch on the light? You've woken the whole house up already.'

'OK, I will then.' Gertie fumbled for the light switch, flicked it on, then promptly switched it off again.

'A whole rack of test-tubes, Gertie. You smashed a whole rack of test-tubes. Mum and Dad will kill you!' Joe whispered in horror.

Gertie was silent for a moment, then: 'They'll think it was the mice,' she said slowly. 'They're always complaining that they chew their notes for nests.'

'Hadn't you better sweep the glass up?' said Joe.

'Since when did mice learn to sweep? Idiot!' Gertie was fuming. She felt like kicking herself but knew she'd probably miss. Instead, she swung the torch beam over the mess.

'Oh no! The dummy's covered! It was blood in the test-tubes. What are we going to do?' she wailed.

'Ssshh!' hissed Joe. 'It's only blood, throwing itself about again.' Then he relented. 'Don't panic, Gertie, it just got his feet. Pity he's got no shoes. There, hold him by the knees and you'll be all right. And don't worry. You can't catch anything, you know. The blood's all cleaned long before Mum and Dad get their hands on it. Now, *please* can we get out of here?'

He shifted his end of the dummy so that its arm was round his neck and its head rested against his shoulder. 'Get your wig out of my eyes,' said Joe, and led the way across the lab as quickly as he could. There were two more labs: the first was crammed with chemicals and the second with computers. They were half-way across this last room, when 'Yikes!' squawked Joe. A small furry thing shot over the floor, through the torch beam and into a dark corner.

'That,' observed Gertie, brightening up a bit, 'was a mouse. A naughty, note-nibbling, test-tube-toppling mouse.' Suddenly she felt less guilty. 'Let me take his top half,' she offered, as Joe fumbled with the handle of the door to the turret. She grasped the mannequin under the arms, Joe opened the door and they stepped through. There was a crash of thunder and a sudden gust of wind slammed the door shut behind them.

'Phew,' whispered Joe. 'Almost there.'

The spiral staircase was narrow and the poor dummy had his head banged mercilessly against the walls on the way up. 'Can't you be careful, Gertie? You're chipping his paintwork.'

'Stop whingeing and open the door,' said Gertie. She watched her brother jam his torch between his teeth and ransack his pockets for the key. 'Hurry up!' Her arms were aching.

'Got it.'

The thunderclap was so close that it shook the turret and made their teeth rattle. Then at last the key clattered in the lock and the door swung open.

11.45 P.M. THURSDAY

Joe and Gertie tipped the mannequin on to the floor and ran to light the lamps.

Only the labs and the middle part of the house, where the Steins lived, had electricity, so the children had set up a ring of powerful torches round the walls of the den. Joe had just turned on the last of these when a brilliant flash of lightning floodlit the room. And there was their dummy, slumped in two halves on the floor, his wig askew and his face buried in the bright red petals of the Indian rug.

'Poor thing,' said Joe. 'Let's put him together.' He had to raise his voice and shout over the thunder that followed fast and furious.

'Careful of his feet,' warned Gertie, 'and there may be glass in his clothes.'

'I'm being careful. That's it. Now, where do we put him?'

'Over here by the window where he can watch the storm.'

Together they propped the dummy up, with his hands on the windowsill and his forehead resting against the cold glass panes. Joe straightened his wig, Gertie smoothed his jacket, and they both stepped back to admire their handiwork.

The lightning took them by surprise. It seemed to leap into the room with them, turning everything a dazzling, brilliant white. Then it was gone, leaving them rubbing their eyes.

'That's funny,' said Gertie. 'There wasn't any thunder.'

Instead there was a loud thud as their dummy toppled to the floor.

'I don't blame you, pal,' said Joe, 'that last lightning flash was a bit much for me too.' He started to rummage in his knapsack. 'I've got the leftovers from tea in here somewhere,' he muttered.

'Joe . . .'

Gertie didn't usually speak so softly. She didn't usually pinch Joe's arm to get his attention, either. And she wasn't usually much of a one for silly expressions and pointing. Now she was doing all four.

12.02 A.M. FRIDAY

'Yes, what is it?' Joe looked up. 'Oh, him. He's only fallen down. We haven't broken him or anything. I'll prop him up again if you like.' He made to get up but Gertie's grip on his arm became positively vice-like.

She pulled him close and thrust her face in his ear. 'He's breathing,' she hissed, severely damaging her brother's eardrum and sorely trying his good temper.

'Just don't start,' snapped Joe. 'You and your creepy stories. I'm not an idiot and you don't spook me that easily.' He shook off Gertie's hand and stood up.

But whatever could that noise be? It wasn't thunder exactly, though it was loud and rolling. And it wasn't one of those banshee howls the wind sometimes makes, though it whistled. There it went again, regular as snoring – deep, throaty snoring.

Joe sat down again, hard, on Gertie's foot. And she didn't even grumble, just resumed her grip on his arm in a let's-stick-together sort of way.

There was a long pause, broken only by the dummy's snores, then suddenly they both began to speak at once, in agitated whispers.

'He's sleeping.'

'Well, let's not wake him up.'

'But we can't leave him there. He hasn't even got a pillow.'

'Don't be stupid. He doesn't need a pillow. He's just a plastic dummy.'

'Those snores sound pretty human to me.'

'OK, a sleeping plastic dummy then.'

'What will happen when he wakes up?'

'I don't want to be here to find out.'

'What will Mum say? And Dad?'

'They mustn't know.'

'We're not certain that he is alive.'

'Of course he's alive. He's snoring, isn't he?'

'But we've got to *do* something!'

'Well, if you want to do something go ahead and do something. I'm quite tired actually. I think I'll go to bed.'

Gertie was getting impatient. 'Don't you dare, Joe Stein,' she said. 'You're staying right here. I'm going to have a closer look. Pass me the torch, I'll bash him over the head with it if he tries any funny business.'

Brandishing the torch like a truncheon, she crept forward. The storm had passed and through the window she could see the moon soaring free of the clouds. The body on the floor certainly looked like their plastic dummy. Then Gertie noticed that his wig had slipped and that the top of his bald head was as smooth and downy-looking as a baby's. His fingers had somehow unstuck themselves from one another and were curled into relaxed fists. Gertie leaned forward and saw that the dummy's face, among the flowers on the carpet, wore a cherubic smile.

She loosened her grip on the torch. 'Oh look, Joe. He's sleeping like a baby!'

'He's taller than Dad, he's made of orange plastic and he's snoring like an engine. How can he be sleeping like a baby?'

'Come and see.'

Gertie was right. There was something very appealing about the crumpled figure on the floor. Joe saw that straight away. He crouched down for a closer look.

'Perhaps we should wake him up after all,' he said.

'Oh, but he looks so happy.'

The dummy gave a deep contented snort.

Very cautiously, Joe reached out and touched one of the smooth, orange hands. 'Skin!' he said in amazement. He squeezed the hand gently and whispered: 'Wake up! It's time to wake up.'

The dummy opened his eyes immediately (revealing a startling blue stare), opened his mouth (revealing a startling absence of teeth), and howled.

Joe leapt several feet backwards and Gertie waved the torch frantically over the creature's head.

'Ssshh! Oh God, Joe, what will we do? He'll wake Mum and Dad. Ssshh!' yelled Gertie and brandished the torch. At once the howls subsided. The blue eyes sparkled with curiosity. The toothless mouth gurgled and drooled. A pair of hands fluttered up into the air, and Gertie and Joe began to relax. The hands danced briefly like butterflies – then seized the torch in an iron grip and shoved it in the toothless mouth.

'Hey!' cried Joe. 'That's our torch! Hey, Mister . . . er, Sir.' He looked at Gertie. 'What do we call him?'

Gertie stared down at the strange figure furiously sucking their torch. Her gaze took in the bare feet, the dusty suit, the frayed tie and came to rest on the join mark, where the dummy's head met his body. Finally, she looked back at Joe and said, with great seriousness, 'Don't you see? There's only one thing we *can* call him.'

'What's that?'

'Franklin, of course. Franklin *Stein*.'

12.22 A.M. FRIDAY

As far as Joe was concerned the whole situation was already well beyond a joke. But if Gertie wanted to call the dummy after some deranged monster from a horror story, he wasn't going to let it upset him. He folded his arms, took a deep breath and gave what he thought was an encouraging smile. 'Please, Franklin, give the torch back before you break it.'

But Franklin had already lost interest. He swung his hand and let go. Fortunately Joe ducked and the wall took the full force of the blow. The torch was dead on arrival.

'Do you think he's got superhuman strength?' asked Gertie, inspecting the damage. Franklin sucked his toes and chirruped. His fingers curled around his tie.

'Watch out, he's going to choke himself!' Joe's head cracked against Gertie's as they lunged to loosen Franklin's tie. But the knot was old and stiff and wouldn't keep still, being attached to a throat that shrieked with laughter whenever someone touched it. There were several broken fingernails before Joe wrenched the tie from Franklin's grasp.

'He's very ticklish,' Joe observed. 'And why does he want to suck every – No! Not my hand! No! Not in your mouth!'

'At least he hasn't any teeth yet,' said Gertie.

Joe wiped his hand on his trouser leg and eyed his sister suspiciously. 'What do you mean "Yet"?' he demanded.

'Don't you see? He's just like a baby. It's as if he's just been born. He hasn't any teeth or hair, he dribbles all the time and he can't speak.'

To be honest, the prospect of caring for a six-foot tall former dummy, with a mental age you could measure in minutes and possibly with super-human strength, filled Joe with . . . well, there isn't really a word for it.

He swallowed hard and said, 'Well, if he can't speak, we'll just have to teach him, double quick.'

'I don't think he can walk, either,' Gertie murmured.

'This is going to be impossible.' Joe glanced at his watch. 'Look, it's one o'clock in the morning. We've got six hours before we have to be in our beds ready to get up. We'll just have to do our best.'

He looked expectantly at Gertie. 'Well? What do we have to do?'

'How should I know?' his sister snapped. 'I've never looked after a baby before. And I'm not even sure I want to start now.' She chewed her lip, then: 'We're going to have to think of something,' she added, staring wildly round the room for inspiration.

Franklin, meanwhile, had found Joe's hand again. 'Mama,' he cooed, and stuffed it in his mouth.

'No, no, not Mama,' said Joe, tearing himself free with some difficulty. 'I'm Joe. That's Gertie. And why don't you suck your own thumb? I'm sure it tastes better than mine.'

'Jogert!' said Franklin agreeably, and thumped himself in the face.

'That's right,' cried Joe. 'Joe, Gertie and' (here he paused for effect and jabbed the former dummy in the chest) 'you Franklin.'

'Stew rank!' returned the echo, enthusiastically, if incorrectly. 'Stew rank Jogert!'

'Got it!' cried Gertie, jumping up and frantically rummaging under the cushions that littered the den. She returned bearing an old picture book, saved from when she was a baby. 'This is what we need,' she said.

So Gertie and Joe patiently worked through *Baby's First Alphabet*, from 'apple' to 'zebra', getting Franklin to look at the pictures and repeat the words after them. It was a long job, partly because they were such thorough teachers and partly because Franklin kept swiping the book and chewing the covers.

At last, when even Gertie had said the word 'zebra' so many times she had forgotten what it meant, they decided to move on to Franklin's physical development.

'Let's see if he can sit up,' Joe suggested. With Gertie pushing his shoulders and Joe hauling on his hands, they levered Franklin into a sitting position. His shoulders sagged and his bald head wobbled precariously, but he didn't fall.

'He almost looks like a businessman,' whispered Gertie, staring in amazement at the tall grey-suited figure before them.

'Ness man!' crowed Franklin and promptly ruined the effect by sticking his thumb in his mouth. Now he was upright, he was able to take a proper look at his surroundings. And what surroundings. Franklin gazed round the room, his eyes big with wonder.

Mr and Mrs Stein would have been equally pop-eyed if they could have seen what their children had done to the turret. (They couldn't, because Gertie and Joe generally locked the door.) The walls were bright with tapestries and mirrors, while vivid rugs and cushions, inlaid chests and trinkets covered the floor. Of course the tapestries were threadbare, the mirrors cracked, the rugs and cushions moth-eaten, the chests riddled with woodworm, and the trinkets battered, but all the same, it was an Ali Baba's cave of a room. In the course of many a midnight raid, the children had plundered the west wing of its finest treasures, carting off anything that caught their eyes and their imagination.

The little round room glittered like a magpie's nest. Franklin liked it.

He hiccuped, rolled over and shot off on all fours, scattering bric-à-brac left and right. Gertie caught her telescope as he tossed it aside, Joe rescued his drawings seconds before they were ripped to shreds, but neither of them was quick enough to save their box of farm animals, which split at the seams under a massive blow from Franklin's elbow. Plastic sheep and cows cascaded across the floor. Franklin paused momentarily to chuck a couple in his mouth, then spotted their cactus collection and was off again.

'Stop him! Stop him!' Gertie yelled. 'He'll wreck the place!'

Joe and Gertie hurled themselves on Franklin. Clinging to his shoulders and worrying him, they were like a couple of terriers trying to divert a bull in its proverbial career across a china shop. 'What, oh what,' thought Gertie frantically, 'is capable of stopping a bull in mid-charge?' Of course! The turret wall. Happy to oblige the wall stepped into the bull's path and converted it into a felled ox. It looked for a moment as though Franklin might cry. The wide mouth gaped, revealing a pair of tonsils and what looked like the beginnings of a large front tooth . . . then closed again in a noisy yawn. The long eyelashes drooped. 'Jogert,' he sighed. 'Stew rank Jogert . . . zebra.'

A loud, unmistakable snore trilled through the room. From the window came the softer but equally unmistakable whistle and trill of the dawn chorus.

Gertie and Joe regarded one another blearily and rose to their feet. Moving about the room on tiptoe, they found a blanket and laid it softly over the sleeping figure. Then they crept to bed. Never in their lives had they stayed up as late as this, which is probably why they forgot to lock the turret door.

7.50 A.M. FRIDAY

A few hours later, when Mrs Stein went into the kitchen, she found her two children and her husband slumped in silence over their breakfast cereal.

'Something really odd has happened,' she said. 'I've just been up to the labs to check on yesterday's experiment and there's a whole rack of test-tubes smashed on the floor. The place looks like a bloodbath.'

Both children suddenly found something fascinating to look at in the bottom of their breakfast bowls.

'Must have been the mice,' said Mr Stein. 'They get everywhere.'

'What kind of blood was it?' Gertie casually asked her cornflakes.

'Oh, just ordinary AB. Bit of a drag, though, having to set up the whole experiment again.' Mrs Stein helped herself to a piece of toast and picked up the morning paper. Joe let her read in peace for a few minutes, but once he judged she was sufficiently distracted 'Mum?' he said in an off-hand, world-weary sort of way.

'Yes, lovey?'

'Er, well . . . How do you look after little babies?' he blurted out.

'Not *little* babies,' corrected Gertie, 'just babies.'

Mrs Stein didn't even look up. 'Oh, it's months of nappies and feeds before you can actually start doing anything interesting with them.'

'Nappies?' gasped Gertie, with something approaching horror.

'Yes, nappies, Gertie,' said Mrs Stein dryly. 'Why this sudden interest in babies?'

'No reason,' said Gertie. 'No reason at all. Except, Mum . . .' her voice rose plaintively. 'I'm feeling rather strange. I've got a headache and, well, I don't think I really ought to go . . .'

'Me too,' groaned Joe.

'Oh, no, you don't,' said Mr Stein, standing up abruptly. 'It's school for both of you. And if you don't run and get your bikes now, you'll be late.'

Reluctantly, Joe and Gertie pedalled down the long road into town.

But school passed like a dream. Joe slept through Maths. Gertie slept through English, and they both slept through Music, thereby saving their teacher the trouble of working out who was singing in the wrong key. 'That's much better,' she said, closing the piano lid on the dot of 3.30. 'Class dismissed.'

Feeling greatly refreshed and ready to face the day, Joe and Gertie were first to get their bikes out of the school shed, and they pedalled up the hill towards home twice as fast as they had pedalled down.

They dropped their bicycles in the hall (a habit which infuriated their parents), clattered up the stairs, along the corridor, and burst into the lab. 'Hi, Mum. Hi, Dad,' they called on their way through.

Mrs Stein paused in her conversation. 'Hi, kids,' she said and turned back to her husband. 'Well,' she said, 'he stepped out right in front of the car. I thought he was hitching a lift, but all I could get out of him was that he was after some stew and yogurt. He was very insistent about the yogurt. So I dropped him off at the supermarket.'

Gertie froze with her hand on the door knob. 'Stew and yogurt . . .' she mouthed silently, 'stew rank Jogert . . .'

'I hope he got what he wanted,' continued Mrs Stein, 'but I don't know what the cashiers will make of him. He really was most odd.'

She looked round. 'Where did those children go? I could have sworn they came in here just a moment ago.'

'They did, and rushed straight out again,' observed her husband. 'But tell me about this chap you met. What was so strange about him?'

'Oh, everything, but what struck me as most

odd was that at one point he actually started to *chew* the car dashboard . . .'

Fortunately the children missed their mother's last remark. Gertie had already yanked Joe out of the room, along the corridor and back down the stairs, and now she had him by his school tie up against the front door. 'You forgot to lock the turret, didn't you!' she hissed accusingly.

'*I* forgot?'

'Yes, *you*! You're the one that insists on looking after the key.' Gertie was never normally as aggressive as this, but then she was never normally consumed with anxiety about a runaway mannequin. Joe didn't feel too good either.

'I was really tired, so I suppose, yes, I did forget,' he conceded, 'but you never reminded me. Anyway,' he shook himself free, 'we'd better start searching for him. He could be anywhere by now.'

'Let's hope he's still in the supermarket,' said Gertie, disentangling her bike, 'otherwise we'll just have to ask people.' She leapt into the saddle and tore up the gravel path, yelling at Joe over her shoulder. 'Hurry! We've got to catch him before he smashes up the whole town.'

They flew back down the hill, past the school, along the high street and skidded to a halt in the supermarket forecourt.

3.50 P.M. FRIDAY

Abandoning their bikes in a heap on the tarmac, Joe and Gertie sidled up to the building and peered through the long glass window at the front.

The checkouts were deserted, the drinks counter was unmanned, shopping trolleys lay abandoned in the aisles. 'Where is everybody?' whispered Joe.

'Over there.' Gertie pointed to a huddle of staff and customers over by the fridges. 'This looks like trouble,' she added huskily, tripping over Joe's heels as she followed him inside.

Somewhere on the far side of the crowd round the dairy display, a forlorn voice requested an apple, a zebra and a violin.

'Oh, no.' Gertie's throat was dry and her hands shook worse than when she had to read a story at morning assembly. She thrust them in her pockets. 'Let's get this over with.'

She stepped forward purposefully, cleared her throat and inquired loudly, 'Is anything the matter?'

Instantly the crowd parted, revealing a familiar figure in a bedraggled grey suit. Franklin sat in the middle of a large, white lake. This, Joe realized with an unpleasant, sinking feeling, was actually the entire contents of the milk, cream and yogurt cabinet. He closed his eyes. 'Wake me up when it's all over,' he muttered.

But Gertie ignored him. She also ignored the swarm of busybodies, the milk puddles, the yogurt smears, and the fact that Franklin had no shoes on and the join marks where his feet met his ankles were clearly on view for all to see. It was all trivia, distractions. The problem was how to shut it out. Gertie pulled herself up to her full height (four foot six to be precise), narrowed her eyes, jabbed her chin in the air, and concentrated on the matter in hand.

'Ah, Franklin . . . *Uncle* Franklin,' she corrected herself. 'There you are. We've been looking all over for you.'

Franklin raised his head, which now wore a fine growth of baby hair and a hefty dollop of cream topping. 'Jogert!' he wailed, catching sight of his friends. He pulled himself to his feet and shambled towards them, splattering careless bystanders with fromage frais.

'Jogert,' cried Franklin, crushing them in a passionate and soggy embrace. At which point Joe was forced to open his eyes. He took one of the outstretched hands and gave it a squeeze. Gertie took the other. 'Well,' she said brightly, 'we must be off.' And they turned to go.

'Excuse me.' The man who stepped in front of them wore a special badge to let people know that he was Mr A. Perkins, supermarket manager. Mr A. Perkins, supermarket manager, had menacing eyes: hard and cold and blue. 'Not so fast!' they flashed. His mouth, however, was much more polite. It merely inquired with a courteous smile, 'Excuse me, do you know this man?'

'Of course we do. He's our uncle,' said Gertie.

There was a brief, expectant pause during which the crowd murmured ominously and Joe and Gertie racked their brains for something else to say. Something that wouldn't involve them in more trouble than they were in already.

'Perhaps we had better discuss this in my office,' suggested Mr A. Perkins, supermarket manager.

'No,' said both the children at once.

'What we mean is,' added Joe, 'we'd love to, but we haven't the time. Poor Uncle Franklin's just had a bad bang on the head and we must get him to a hospital.'

But Perkins swept aside their objections. 'Kindly step this way,' he murmured, ushering them past the baked bean display and the frozen chickens, and into a poky office at the back of the shop.

No sooner were they all crammed in, than he snapped the door shut and stepped behind his desk. 'Right,' he snarled, dropping the polite expression. 'I want an explanation and I want compensation – that (in case they don't teach you brats anything at school) means money to repair the wreckage *your* uncle has caused to *my* shop.'

'We know what compensation is,' Joe cut in.

But Perkins silenced him with a regal gesture. 'Otherwise . . .' he paused, and drew the telephone towards him across his desk. 'Otherwise I call the police.'

'Telephone!' crowed Franklin, who had finally recognized something out of *Baby's First Alphabet*. He tapped Joe's shoulder, grinned and pointed: 'Telephone, Jogert.'

'Yes, it's a telephone,' said Joe. He stared sullenly at the supermarket manager. 'Mum says it's silly to cry over a bit of spilt milk,' he observed.

'A *bit* of spilt milk!' exploded Mr Perkins. He picked up the telephone and began to dial.

'Oh no! Please don't!' cried Gertie. 'I'm sure we'll be able to compensate you.'

Perkins replaced the receiver and pressed the tips of his fingers together. 'I'm waiting,' he drawled.

'We've got five pounds saved up between us,' said Gertie. 'And it's Joe's birthday next week so we'll have at least another tenner then . . .'

Perkins gave a snort of derision. 'I hardly think that fifteen pounds will cover the damage caused by this . . . this moronic freak,' he sneered.

Joe was outraged. 'How dare you call our uncle a moronic freak!' he yelled. 'Come on Gertie, Franklin. We're going. Let him call the police if he wants to.'

'Oh, no, you don't.' Perkins leapt to bar the door, but Gertie who always let her feet do exactly what they wanted – was too fast for him. She tripped him up, quite by accident of course, and Perkins stumbled. Then everything happened very fast.

Afterwards, the children agreed that Perkins must have grabbed at Franklin to stop himself from falling. It was a small room, and rather dark. Everyone was trying to get out of everyone else's way, a chair was knocked over and, in the middle of it all, Perkins seemed to yank at Franklin's hand. There was a sudden sharp metallic sound and Franklin yelped. His hand shot out of his jacket sleeve. Just his hand. Not his wrist, nor his arm, nor any of the rest of his body.

It was Gertie who broke the electric silence that followed.

'Look what you've done! You've pulled off Uncle Franklin's hand!' she cried indignantly. 'How could you?'

4.05 P.M. FRIDAY

There were several possible answers to this question, but Mr A. Perkins, supermarket manager, didn't feel ready to admit to any of them. He was staring in disbelief at the patch of empty air that had suddenly appeared at the end of Franklin's wrist. Slowly he turned his head and examined his own hands. Strangely enough, he now seemed to have three of them. With a shriek of horror he hurled one into his wastepaper bin and fell down in a dead faint.

'Stew rank?' muttered Franklin uncertainly, examining the stump at the end of his arm, out of which protruded a long metal screw.

He lumbered over to the wastepaper basket and retrieved his errant limb. 'Stew rank?' he asked again, and waved it under Gertie's nose.

Now it's one thing to watch a dummy being dismantled in a shop window, with hands, arms or even its head missing. Quite another to watch someone you're already introducing to people as your uncle suddenly part company with a bit of his body. It takes some getting used to.

Joe was the first to get used to it. As soon as he realized that there wasn't a drop of blood in sight, nor likely to be, he leapt into action.

'Quick!' he hissed.'Quick, before Perkins comes round.'

'Hmm?' mumbled Gertie. She absently patted the hand Franklin held out to her. 'Don't worry, pet,' she said in the voice her father used for grazed knees and splinters. 'We'll have that fixed in a jiffy.'

'There,' she said, taking the hand and screwing it back into place. 'Now you're as right as rain.'

'Bandages!' exclaimed Joe. 'What we need is bandages. Gertie take off your socks!'

Gertie opened her mouth to object and discovered she was too dazed to argue. So she sat down in the deep, leather chair behind the manager's desk and meekly removed her socks.

'Right,' said Joe, binding Gertie's white knee length socks over the thin line that marked where Franklin's hand was joined to Franklin's wrist. 'Now we need some blood.'

'Not real blood,' he added hastily. 'Just any old red stuff.'

Gertie opened the top drawer of the desk and peered inside.

'There's a lot of funny stuff in here,' she said, stirring the contents with her hand. 'Candles . . . cards . . . Oh, look, there's a crystal ball – would that be any use?'

'Something red and wet, Gertie,' her brother reminded her.

Gertie slammed the drawer shut and opened the one beneath. 'Ah,' she said. 'Here it is.' And she passed Joe a large pot of red ink.

'Great.' Joe opened the pot and tipped a generous amount over the bandage, and a slightly less generous amount over the carpet besides. 'There. That looks pretty realistic. In fact it's making me pretty sick just looking at it.' He handed the pot back to Gertie. 'Hide it in his drawer.'

'Fine,' said Gertie, who hadn't the least idea what Joe was up to, but was happy to go along with anything if it kept her out of a police cell. 'What now?' she asked.

'Now to stop Perkins making trouble.' Joe knelt over the fainting man and said loudly:

'Mr Perkins!'

Perkins flinched.

'My uncle has been good enough to say that he won't press charges,' said Joe, 'so that phone call to the police won't be necessary.'

'Charges? Police?' Perkins sat up abruptly and rubbed his head. 'I'm sorry, but I don't understand . . .' he said weakly.

'But Mr Perkins, don't you remember what happened?' Joe looked meaningfully at Franklin's makeshift bandage. Perkins followed his gaze.

'Your uncle's hand!' he yelped. 'What did I do to his hand?'

Gertie was catching on now. 'It's OK, Mr Perkins. It's only . . .' she searched for the correct expression, 'a flesh wound. But the shock, you know. I don't know whether our poor uncle will ever recover from your vicious attack . . .'

Franklin beamed wetly and waved his bandaged paw, knocking the overhead light and setting it dancing madly.

Perkins put his hand over his eyes. 'I . . . I . . . I don't know what to say,' he finished lamely.

'Don't say anything,' said Gertie, patting him reassuringly on the shoulder. 'And don't worry, there's no need to get up. We'll show ourselves out.'

It was as if someone had pressed the rewind button on a video player: the frozen chickens, the baked beans, the dairy produce, the checkouts all flashed past at high speed, and then Gertie, Joe and Franklin spilled out into the car park and collapsed in relief against a wall.

4.10 P.M. FRIDAY

Joe was clutching his stomach. 'Did I just do what I think I did?' he asked.

'You did,' said Gertie. 'You were fiendishly brilliant. And, as long as you don't brag about it,' she added generously, 'I'm prepared to forget that the whole thing was your fault in the first place, for leaving the turret door unlocked.'

'At least Franklin's safe,' said Joe. They both grinned at their friend, who had just discovered the dollop of cream in his hair.

'Jogert,' he said, offering them some.

'No thanks,' said Gertie. '*Uncle* Franklin,' and she fell about laughing. 'Oh,' she gasped, and hugged herself. 'I'm so glad we got out of that one.'

Suddenly her eyes narrowed and she turned back to Joe. 'How come,' she said, her hands on her hips, 'how come I had to take my socks off and you didn't? Mum'll kill me. I bet those ink stains don't come out.'

'Because I'm wearing the Mickey Mouse ones Dad got me,' her brother snapped.

Gertie thought for a moment, decided it was a satisfactory explanation, and plonked herself down beside Joe on the wall.

Meanwhile Franklin inspected the nearest car, which chanced to be the large and shiny red Mercedes belonging to one Mr A. Perkins, supermarket manager. He ambled round it, peering at the headlights and jabbing at the bonnet. Finally he got down on his hands and knees to investigate the creature's feet. 'Wheel!' he cooed, recognizing another word out of *Baby's First Alphabet*. He grasped the right front wheel in both hands and tugged. Something underneath the car gave, and suddenly Franklin was crashing backwards on to the tarmac.

Gertie and Joe spun round. 'What's going on?'

'Wheel, Jogert,' announced Franklin, holding up a particularly large and shiny example for them to admire.

'We can't take our eyes off you for one second!' Gertie yelled in exasperation. 'Put that wheel back, Franklin. Put it back at once!'

Joe put out his hand to stop her. 'Don't shout at him. He's still only a baby.' But it was too late. Franklin clutched the wheel to his chest and bawled. His eyes spouted tears like a fountain. His face turned the same shade of red as Perkins's car. Joe and Gertie gaped.

They had never even heard of toddler tantrums

before, let alone witnessed one at close quarters. If the noise was deafening, the sight of Franklin kicking – and denting – the tarmac was even more unnerving.

'What will we do?' whispered Gertie.

But Joe was at a loss for words.

So it was Gertie who braved the thrashing legs and flailing fists to get close enough to put her arm round Franklin. 'I'm sorry,' she said. 'I'm sorry I shouted.' She had to repeat this a good many times before the yells subsided. Then she tried to explain, against a barrage of hiccups, that the wheel didn't belong to him and he'd have to put it back.

But 'Franklin wheel,' he insisted. He looked at the children's bicycles. 'Jogert wheel,' he pointed out, 'Franklin wheel.' He sniffed stubbornly.

The logic of this defeated them. Too weary to argue, Joe and Gertie picked up their bicycles and, with Franklin and his new toy wedged firmly between them, set off for home.

They went the long way round because, as Gertie pointed out, it wouldn't do to be spotted on the main road. It was quite a walk, but once the town was well behind them, the children forgot all about wrecked cars and smashed supermarkets. The sun was shining, birds sang in the hedgerows and Franklin gambolled along beside them like a playful buffalo.

They let him help lift their bikes over the stile into the daisy meadow, and narrowly stopped him diving over head first himself. 'Cow!' he cried, and, 'Flower, Jogert!' He wore a wide, gap-toothed grin. He was beside himself with excitement, crouching down in the long grass to introduce Gertie to a daisy. And as he insisted on doing this with every flower he saw, their progress across the meadow was painfully slow. 'Let's teach him to count,' Gertie said at last. And she sat him down and proceeded to teach him his numbers.

'He's learning really fast,' she told Joe, as Franklin wandered off in search of his two-hundred-and-forty-second daisy.

Joe nodded. 'Yes, and he's getting some teeth now . . . Have you noticed, though, he doesn't seem to need to eat.'

'Well,' said Gertie. 'At least that gets rid of the problem of feeds and nappies.'

Sitting there in the daisy meadow, watching Franklin chase the cows, all their difficulties seemed to evaporate in the afternoon sun.

'We can teach him to talk properly,' said Joe, idly spinning Franklin's wheel.

'Yes, and he can live in the turret . . .'

'And we'll get him anything he needs out of the west wing.'

So they whiled away the afternoon making

plans, until at last their stomachs reminded them that they, at least, had to eat.

'Twenty-three cow, fifty-six hundred seventy-three flower,' Franklin informed them happily when they rounded him up.

'Twenty-three cows and . . . let me see, that's five thousand, six hundred and seventy-three daisies,' corrected Gertie. 'What? In this big bunch?' She looked round the meadow. 'Oh Franklin, you've picked them all, you idiot.'

'Just be grateful the cows wouldn't let him pick them too,' said Joe. 'Come on, let's go before he starts counting blades of grass. Hey, Franklin, don't forget your wheel.'

6.58 P.M. FRIDAY

'Tea's burnt, you dirty stop-outs!' shouted their father from the kitchen as they sneaked in the back door.

'There in a minute,' promised Joe and Gertie, as they bundled Franklin up the stairs.

But it took them fully a quarter of an hour to get Franklin settled in his turret room.

'That suit's revolting, and it's beginning to smell,' remarked Gertie, who had been considering giving Franklin a goodnight hug but decided against it. 'How are we ever going to get it clean?'

'We can bung it in the washing-machine when Mum and Dad go to bed,' suggested Joe. 'It'll be ready by the morning.'

So Franklin modestly removed his clothes behind the large green towel Joe held up for him. 'Not that there's anything to hide,' confided Joe. 'After all, he's not like you or me. He's a shop dummy.'

He wound the towel tight round Franklin's waist. 'That's it,' he said. 'Now we've got to go, or Dad will kill us.'

Gertie opened the door. 'We've got to eat our tea, Franklin,' she explained. 'After that, we'll have to have baths and entertain Mum and Dad for a bit and then we can go to bed. Which means we'll come back and see you. OK?'

'You won't try to escape, will you?' They both pointed at the open doorway and back at Franklin, shaking their heads firmly. 'No open door, Franklin.'

'No,' agreed Franklin. He too shook his head gravely.

'Cheerio then.'

'Cheer oh Jogert,' replied Franklin, and they closed the door behind them.

As the sound of departing feet faded in the distance, Franklin stared at the locked door and continued shaking his head. Suddenly his eyes took on a curious, fixed expression. He raised his hands to his ears and gave his head an experimental twist.

9.17 P.M. FRIDAY

When Gertie and Joe returned they found three things that demanded their immediate attention.

The first of these was the broken lock on the door to their den.

The second was the room itself. It appeared to have been completely stripped. There was nothing there. No tapestries. No rugs. No mirrors. Only a curious grey rubble that covered the floor. Joe cautiously disturbed it with his toe and it fell apart in a jumble of marbles, decks of cards, draughtsmen, tiddlywinks, jigsaw pieces, books and bits of broken glass.

'This is what it's like after an earthquake,' thought Gertie.

They were standing, slumped in the doorway, shining their torches over the wreckage, when their attention was riveted by a sight more awful than anything they had yet experienced. It was Franklin's head, sitting bang in the middle of his wheel, blinking.

'Jogert!' wailed the head pathetically. 'Oh Jogert, no body.' This was as far as Franklin's limited vocabulary would allow him to go, so he rolled his eyes expressively and let Joe and Gertie do the talking. Which they did.

'Oh Franklin how could you?' they demanded. 'What have you done to our room? Where's your body gone?' There was, of course, a whole lot more, mostly to do with what they thought about people who broke other people's things. But, fortunately, they spoke very fast and both at the same time, so most of it went right over Franklin's head. But, if he couldn't understand a word they were saying, at least he could pretend. So he half-closed his eyes, smiled faintly, and generally tried to look knowing.

Gertie immediately put down her torch. 'He hasn't the faintest idea what we're talking about, poor thing,' she said.

But Joe wasn't so sure. He picked his way across the rubble and squatted down beside the wheel. 'Franklin, did you do this?' he asked, waving his hand above the wreckage on the floor.

The head looked completely taken aback. 'No,' it said in a shocked voice. It flashed Joe a reproachful look and then said decisively, 'Body do.' And it turned its eyes up to the ceiling as if its body were a badly behaved child and it the embarrassed parent.

'I didn't suppose you bashed all our things up

with your head,' snapped Joe. 'Of course it was your body. But it was still you.'

'And if we had any sense, we'd make you clear the whole lot up,' added Gertie. She glared at the head until its bottom lip began to quiver dangerously, then, 'OK,' she sighed. 'You're not up to it at the moment, so we'll do it. But just this once, mind.'

She bent down and started picking some of the rubbish off the floor. 'We mustn't panic,' she muttered. 'We must think straight. It's the middle of the night, our den's been wrecked and . . .' she broke off, looking at Joe.

'At least the window isn't broken,' he remarked. It was the only positive thing he could think of to say.

'Our den's wrecked,' Gertie went on, 'and as I was going to say before I was so rudely interrupted: *there's a headless maniac loose in the house*.'

'A naked, headless maniac,' corrected Joe. 'Unless of course he's still wearing the towel. But I don't see any reason why he'd keep that on, if he can't even keep his head on.'

Gertie suddenly gave up trying to clear the room. 'This is useless,' she said, letting a handful of marbles bounce back into the rubble. She clambered over to the wheel, picked up Franklin's head and tucked it underneath her arm.

'Jogert,' murmured the head.

'If you could only see how awful that looks,' her brother observed drily.

'Well we can't just leave him sitting there.'

'Why not? His body did,' retorted Joe.

'Body,' grunted Franklin, from Gertie's armpit.

'Quick, Gertie, he's trying to say something!'

'Seeing he only knows two dozen words and half of those are animals and fruit, he's not going to be able to tell us anything we don't know already,' snapped Gertie. All the same, she held the head out where they could see it. 'Yes, Franklin?' she asked.

But it looked as if she was right about Franklin's poor language skills. 'Body no Perkins. Body cow,' was all he could come up with. They considered this for some time and could make nothing of it. It was like one of the clues to those impossible crosswords you get on the back page of the newspaper. Joe had a feeling that the answer would be something like 'wellington boot' or 'refrigerator'. He was still racking his brains when Gertie gave up.

'Tell us about the body, Franklin. What do you mean?' she asked.

Franklin tried again. 'Body no . . .' and here he screwed his face into a hideously evil leer. 'Body . . .' he said again, and this time he let his jaw drop and his tongue loll.

'Got it!' cried Joe, snapping his fingers under Franklin's nose so that the head crossed its eyes in confusion. 'What he means is that his body isn't horrible, like Perkins, it's just a bit thick, like a cow.'

'Great, that really puts my mind at rest,' said Gertie, 'knowing it's only a headless cow rampaging through the house.'

Joe looked at her. 'I suppose we're going to have to find it,' he groaned.

'Yes,' said Gertie shortly. 'And we'd better start now.' She turned to Franklin's head. 'Sorry,' she explained, 'but I need my hands free to hold my torch and I'm sure you don't want to be left behind.' And, with that, she shoved it in her knapsack.

'Apple,' mumbled the head, surprised to find itself suddenly sharing a small space with one.

10.22 P.M. FRIDAY

They decided to start with the attics, which stretched the entire length of the house, from the east gable to the west, forming a long, dark tunnel under the eaves. It was a creaky, eerie place, full of small scuttling creatures and scattered with puddles of moonlight, which poured in through holes in the roof. Gertie and Joe liked to think of it as an Amazonian rainforest, and of themselves as explorers. But tonight they weren't in the mood. They crept along with their heads down, to avoid fluttering bats, and their arms well out in front of them, to push aside the sticky curtains of cobweb. By the time they finally reached the west gable, they were all of a jump and a shudder.

'Thank goodness that's over,' breathed Joe, fumbling for the trap-door. He pulled it open and leapt down into the black pit below.

'Careful with Franklin's head,' he called. 'We don't want him to get hurt. Here, pass him down to me.'

He reached up and grabbed the knapsack, then stood back to let Gertie drop down through the trap-door, her torch clenched between her teeth like a pirate's cutlass.

'Ow!' cried Gertie, landing badly and jarring her spine. 'I think I've cracked a tooth.' A good five minutes were wasted while she examined her mouth for dental damage. 'All clear,' she finally announced, and they set off again.

Slowly they worked their way through all four floors of the west wing, shining their torches into old wardrobes and under brass bedsteads, over trunks, behind bookcases and inside rusty old deep-freezes. But of Franklin's body there was no sign, not so much as a finger.

They called a halt on the ground floor, in front of an open door, out of which a steady stream of clammy air escaped, like breath from a gaping mouth. 'I don't think he's been here,' said Joe. 'Nothing's been disturbed.' He swung his torch. 'See, the only footprints in the dust are ours.'

'Let's try the cellars then,' said Gertie, and she led the way through the door and down a dank stone staircase. The cellars were wet. They were always wet, but last night's downpour meant that the children soon found themselves up to their ankles in a sludgy mixture of mud and water. Gertie set her jaw and waded on, trying not to imagine what creatures (leeches? rats?) might be swirling around her feet. Joe followed, shining his torch over the streaky stone walls.

'It's like a dungeon in here,' he said, and his voice echoed grandly in the wide, black spaces beyond their torch beams.

Gertie swung round. 'Don't do that,' she yelled. 'It's horrible!' And her voice, too, boomed from wall to wall like thunder.

'Horrible!' bellowed the echo.

And from its position upside down in Gertie's knapsack, its nose flattened painfully against an apple, Franklin's head began to wail.

This was really too much. The children splashed wildly through the water, racing for the far door.

Joe hauled it open, Gertie clanged it shut behind them, and they both collapsed back against it in relief.

'Right,' said Gertie, once she had got her breath back. 'I don't care what Franklin's body is doing, because my body has got to recover. Let's go and have a snack in the kitchen.'

'Do you think Mum and Dad will be in bed yet?' said Joe.

'Of course they will. It's almost midnight.'

Gertie was right. The grandfather clock in the hall was striking twelve as they switched on the kitchen light and sank down gratefully round the kitchen table. The bright, familiar room and the smell of their tea-time spaghetti made them feel better at once.

'Let's see what there is to eat,' said Joe. He

reached over and swung the fridge door open. 'Ugh! I wish Mum and Dad would store their blood samples somewhere else. None of my friends at school have to put up with this sort of thing. It's disgusting!' And he turned away. 'I wasn't hungry anyway,' he said.

'You've got to eat to keep your strength up,' Gertie insisted, helping herself to bread, cheese, and the salad for tomorrow's lunch. 'Hey,' she mumbled, through a triple-decker sandwich, 'we might as well put Franklin's clothes in the washing-machine while we're here.'

Without a word, Joe took off his knapsack and pulled out Franklin's suit. 'Have you got my socks there?' his sister asked. Joe produced the ink-stained socks.

'Well, put them in too.'

The bundle of clothing was duly shoved in the washing-machine, and Gertie set it to boil-wash. 'Just to make sure it comes out clean,' she said.

The machine started on its cycle with a warm whooshing sound. Joe slumped against it. 'Now what?' he asked grumpily. He was starving.

Gertie swung her knapsack on to her shoulder with a cheery grin. She felt much better. 'I suppose it will have to be the east wing – that means the labs as well,' she said. 'And then, if we still haven't found it, we'll have to come back and search all the rooms in the main block.'

Joe squared his shoulders and picked up his torch. 'Come on let's get it over with,' he said and led the way up to the labs.

In a room on the second floor of the main block, Mr Stein suddenly sat up in bed.

12.13 P.M. FRIDAY

'Damn it. I forgot to brush my teeth,' said Mr Stein.

His wife glanced up from her bedtime book. 'Get me a glass of water while you're at it, Jim,' she murmured.

So Mr Stein climbed out of bed, picked up the glass on the beside table, walked across the room and opened the door. His timing was perfect. James B. Stein M.Sc. Ph.D., and an alphabet of other qualifications, was able to enjoy a sensational view of something he knew to be impossible.

Sensational, because the headless man trod on his foot as he blundered blindly past.

The obvious thing to do was to leap backwards, shut the door and pretend it hadn't happened. Mr Stein did so. He stood for a few moments, examined the paintwork on the door, which was a nasty shade of yellow, peered at his big toenail, which was beginning to turn black, glanced over his shoulder at his wife, who was still reading her book, and tried again. This time he opened the door more slowly. Ah, the apparition had disappeared. Thankfully he stepped out into the corridor.

The man should have been on the stage. His timing was impeccable. The headless body had crashed into the door at the other end of the passage and was now on its way back, knocking the family portraits askew as it came, and rucking up the carpet with its spade-like feet.

'Excuse me. Excuse me,' said Mr Stein and he fluttered the empty glass in the air to ward the thing off. But, eyeless, earless and utterly brainless, still it bore down on him. James B. Stein M.Sc., Ph.D., etc. was about to become a loss to science when the carpet intervened and tripped the thing up.

The body crashed to the floor at Mr Stein's feet, twitched a couple of times and lay still.

This gave Mr Stein ample opportunity to observe the familiar-looking green towel that the creature sported about its waist and the large screw that protruded from its neck. He suddenly decided that he had seen enough. Moving as daintily as was possible, given his state of mind, Mr Stein edged round until his back was pressed against the bedroom door and fumbled behind him for the door knob. He found it and was about to beat a retreat when a hand closed round his ankle. Mr Stein considered screaming. The hand shifted to his knee and then another grasped his wrist. Mr Stein decided he was definitely going to scream. He was just opening his mouth to do so when the creature bashed him hard under the chin with one of its shoulders as it hauled itself to its feet. Mr Stein bit his tongue.

The glass, which happened to be made of a shatter-proof plastic material, plummeted to the floor and made a lot of noise about not breaking.

'What's going on out there?' called Mrs Stein from the bedroom.

Just at that moment, the door at the end of the corridor opened a crack then pulled itself hastily to. On the far side, Gertie was clutching her panicking heart. 'That's Mum's voice!' she gasped.

'Sshh,' hissed Joe. 'She must have heard us, switch off your torch.'

In the corridor beyond, Franklin's body had Mr Stein's hand in a grasp that was to leave bruises for days. It clung to him like a drunk clinging to a lamp-post, steadying itself for the long stagger home. At last it was ready. The headless man gave Mr Stein's hand a final squeeze, as if to say: 'Thanks, mate,' and lurched off down the passage.

Crouching, with their ears to the closed door, Joe and Gertie heard their father's voice – a little higher pitched than usual, to be sure, but still their father's voice – saying, 'It's nothing, darling.'

Mr Stein picked up the plastic beaker, went back into the bedroom, rummaged in his sock drawer and unearthed a small bottle of whisky from which he took a long, hard swig. Having emptied the rest of the bottle into the beaker, he walked across to his wife and held it out to her. 'Take this, Jill. You're going to need it,' he said. 'I know it's incredible, but I've just seen a ghost . . .'

Joe and Gertie might have been on the other side of the world for all they knew of their father's ordeal.

'Well at least that saves us some work,' said Joe. He switched on his torch and pointed it at the closed door. 'Like Dad said, there's nothing there.'

'Good,' said Gertie. 'We'll do the turrets next.' By the time they reached the last turret, they were both exhausted. 'Nothing here,' said Joe, shining his torch around the small, circular room. And he stamped around a bit to cover the sound of his stomach rumbling.

'My feet are killing me,' moaned Gertie, sitting down abruptly on the bare wooden floor. 'Can't we have a rest?' She took off her knapsack and opened it. 'Excuse me, Franklin, can I have my apple?' she asked politely. 'We haven't found your body yet, by the way.'

While Gertie bit into her apple with gusto, Joe paced the room. The munching sound was setting his teeth on edge. 'Can't you do that more quietly?' he snapped and went and stood as far away as possible, which happened to be by the window. He glanced out. It was a cloudless night with a ghostly stillness to it, which is probably why the headless man leaning with his elbows on the garden gate looked so at home.

Headless man?

Joe spun on his heel. 'You'll never guess who's outside,' he said.

1.02 A.M. SATURDAY

Joe and Gertie took the spiral staircase two steps at a time, tore through the house, and dashed out across the garden.

'Where is he?' panted Gertie, racing over the moonlit lawn.

'Over by the gate,' called Joe.

But the gate, when they reached it, flapped emptily on its hinges.

'I'm sure he was here,' said Joe, peering under the hedge and shining his torch into the rose bushes. 'Phew! I'm boiling after all that,' he added, and pulled off his jumper.

'He can't have gone far,' said Gertie. She tossed her apple core into a bush and walked out of the gate and into the lane. Joe followed after, clutching his jumper with one hand and his stomach with the other. 'It's not good to run on an empty tummy,' he groaned.

'Hush,' said Gertie. She had stopped in the middle of the lane and was looking around. 'What's that noise?' she asked.

'It's only Daisy's gate,' said Joe. 'It needs oiling.'

Daisy, or Miss Roberts, as she preferred to be known, was a bishop's niece and their next-door neighbour. She lived in a pretty cottage, tucked away behind a tall beech hedge and a high wooden gate, which at this particular moment was swinging gently back and forth without any apparent help from the wind. Gertie and Joe stared at it, then raised their eyes and peered into the garden beyond. Just as they thought: there was their runaway, lumbering up the path towards their neighbour's front door.

Joe was horror-struck. 'He's not going to ring the doorbell is he? Daisy will have a heart attack.'

But no, at the last possible moment, Miss Daisy Roberts was saved by her own front doorstep – a stubborn, stout-hearted article much like its owner, which bravely stood its ground against the intruder. Franklin's body knew when it was beaten. Having stubbed both big toes on the step, it keeled over into the flowerbed which lay thoughtfully on hand to receive it.

'Quick! Now's our chance.' Joe and Gertie sprinted up the path and threw themselves down among the snapdragons and pansies.

'Right, let's get his head back on and get him out of here,' hissed Joe.

While Gertie fiddled with the drawstrings on her knapsack, Joe flattened the flowers, jumping from one foot to the other in agitation. 'Hurry! Hurry!'

They were both far too preoccupied to notice the front door of the house open.

'I'm being as fast as I can,' hissed Gertie, sticking her hand in the knapsack and her thumb in Franklin's eye.

Someone cleared their throat loudly.

'Shut up, can't you! You'll wake Daisy,' Gertie spluttered.

Then someone spoke.

'Gertrude! Joseph! What on earth are you doing here?'

Quick as lightning Joe tossed his jumper over the body's neck, over the space where one might reasonably expect its head to be.

'Er, nothing, Miss Roberts,' said Gertie, hurriedly removing her thumb from Franklin's eye and retying the knapsack.

Miss Daisy Roberts stood on her front doorstep and peered down at Joe and Gertie. She had left her spectacles indoors but she was still able to make out the pair of bare legs (too large, surely, to belong to either of the Stein children?) that jutted over her front path.

She stepped forward for a closer look.

'Who on earth is that?' she said, indicating the legs, the green towel and Joe's pullover with a wide sweep of her hand.

'Oh! oh, it's . . . it's Mr Perkins,' said Gertie desperately, saying the first name that came into her head A-A-A-*Anthony* Perkins,' she elaborated.

'Why is he wearing only a towel?' Miss Roberts demanded.

'Maybe his suit's in the wash,' said Joe. He, at least, was trying to be truthful.

'And what's he doing in my flowerbed?' continued Miss Roberts.

'We're not quite sure,' said Joe, playing for time.

The bishop's niece sniffed. There was something fishy going on. She decided to widen her field of inquiry. Lowering herself carefully to her knees, and tucking her blue velveteen slippers beneath her, she regarded the two guilty faces with dignity.

'What,' she said, and paused for emphasis . . . 'What exactly is going on?' and she suddenly looked Gertie straight in the eye.

'You tell me, Gertrude.'

Poor Gertie stared stupidly back. She wondered whether Miss Roberts knew about their midnight raids on her apple tree. She wondered whether Miss Roberts knew they called her Daisy behind her back. She wondered whether the whole thing was a bad dream and she wondered whether, if she tried hard enough, she could make herself wake up. But she never for a moment wondered whether to tell the truth. It was unthinkable. No, they had to save Franklin, both body and head, and if that meant lying, so be it.

So she took a deep breath and said: 'Honestly, Daisy – I mean, Miss Roberts – we just saw him walking up the lane. We recognized him from the supermarket, you see. He works there. So we followed him and then he lay down in your flower-bed . . .'

At last, and not before time, Gertie had a flash of inspiration. She raised her eyebrows and lowered her voice. 'I think he might be drunk,' she said.

'A drunkard!' exclaimed the bishop's niece with a disapproving snort. She paused for a moment to digest this information, before proceeding. 'And what, might I ask, are you children doing out at this time of night?'

'We were,' and here Gertie looked truly ashamed at the depths of the lie she was about to tell, 'we were coming to see if any of the apples were ready on your tree.'

'At last something that has the unmistakable ring of truth about it,' Miss Roberts sighed. She stood up abruptly and brushed the earth off her knees. 'I really don't know what to say. Some drunken shop assistant wanders into my garden in the middle of the night, wearing nothing but a bath towel . . . I really ought to call the police.'

Joe was appalled by this sudden turn of events:

'But Daisy – Miss Roberts – you can't!' He broke off. There was every reason to believe that Miss Roberts could and would. And no doubt the call would have been made and the police summoned, had not Franklin's head seized the chance to join the conversation.

'Daisy!' called a muffled voice from inside the knapsack. 'Five thousand, six hundred and seventy-three daisy, twenty-three cows.'

'I beg your pardon?' said Miss Roberts, looking around wildly.

'It's Mr Perkins,' said Gertie, leaning back heavily against the knapsack. 'I told you he was drunk.'

'Well, he's certainly not sleeping it off in my flowerbed,' snapped Miss Roberts, and she gave the body a good no-nonsense prod with the toe of her slipper. 'Wake up, Perkins! Wake up at once!' she said.

'Body no Perkins, body cow,' insisted Franklin from within the knapsack.

'Eh?' said Miss Roberts. 'The man must be mad.'

'And why's he got a jumper on his head?' she suddenly demanded. And she snatched up the offending article.

There was nothing for it. Joe gave way to hysteria. 'No! Daisy, No!' he shrieked, hurling himself on the bishop's niece, who also happened to be a member of the Abstinence Society and president of the Women's Guild. Not at all the sort of person you grab by the shoulders and shake. But Joe was beyond social niceties. 'You mustn't!' he yelled, his eyes wide with panic. 'We didn't want to tell you but he's not all there, you see. He's lost his head!'

Now this really was something. The child was clearly frightened out of his wits.

'Joseph dear, whatever's the matter?' cried Miss Roberts, all of a flutter and dropping the pullover back where it belonged. 'Did Mr Perkins upset you? Was he acting oddly? What am I saying? Of course he was acting oddly, running around the countryside in a bath towel. Oh you poor dear,' she cried in concern, 'you come inside with me and have a nice glass of water.' And she took Joe firmly by the hand.

'Gertrude,' she instructed. 'Don't you go near that nasty man. Stand over here on the steps and keep an eye on him. I shall telephone the police at once.' And with that she led Joe into the house.

Fortunately it took Miss Roberts some time to track down her spectacles, help Joe to a glass of water and look up the number of the local police station. She was sitting with the phone in her lap, her finger poised above the dial, when Gertie burst in.

'He's gone!' cried Gertie. 'He just got up and went. No need to phone the police.'

Miss Roberts put the receiver down and gave Gertie a searching look.

'I expect,' Gertie continued brightly, 'he just needed a bit of time to gather himself together.' She glanced at Joe. 'You know, get his head screwed on. He's probably on his way home by now.'

Suddenly the bishop's niece felt very weary. She couldn't quite put her finger on it, but those Stein children were up to something. Well they could jolly well stop being up to something on her property.

'If that is the case, Gertrude,' she said, 'I really think you children ought to go home to bed.' She rose stiffly from her chair and showed them to the door. Oh, and there was one other thing. She raised her hand to call them back. 'I'm afraid I'm going to have to have a word with your parents about this,' she said.

But Joe and Gertie were already half-way home and out of earshot.

9.59 A.M. SATURDAY

After twenty-four hours of non-stop wanton destruction Franklin, for one, needed a rest. Likewise Joe and Gertie, who were both suffering from acute nervous exhaustion. As for their parents, they had spent most of the night arguing about the nature of the universe and, more particularly, the existence of ghosts. They were worn out.

So the mice and the bats had the house to themselves, except that they generally slept during the day anyway and didn't intend to break the habits of a lifetime.

It was ten o'clock before anything stirred. Anything in this case being Mrs Stein, who rolled over, poked her husband in the back and demanded to know whether he had come to his senses yet. A few minutes later Joe's stomach shrieked so loudly that its owner catapulted out of bed, yelling, 'Look out, a head!' And scarcely thirty seconds after that Gertie, who was dreaming she was inside a washing-machine, found herself suddenly on the spin cycle being shaken awake.

In the turret, Franklin slumbered on among the rubble, untroubled by empty stomachs, hungry brothers or worries about the supernatural. His thumb slipped from his mouth as he drifted into another dream. He hugged the shiny chrome and rubber wheel close and, softly, he began to burble *Baby's First Alphabet*.

Downstairs in the kitchen things were less relaxed.

'Jim, you're a scientist, not a sausage!' said Mrs Stein, stabbing the loaf viciously with the bread knife. 'You don't believe in ghosts.'

But Mr Stein was sticking to his story. 'I'm telling you, it was a ghost,' he protested. 'A headless ghost. It crushed my big toe and pulverized my hand. Here, I've got the bruises to prove it.' He slammed the tea-pot down on the table, tore off his slipper and brandished his blackened toenail under his wife's nose.

'Morning, kids,' he added, as Joe and Gertie came in for breakfast.

Mrs Stein inspected her husband's foot. 'Good morning,' she said, without looking up. 'Or at least it would be if your father hadn't taken complete leave of his senses.'

Joe and Gertie slid into their chairs and eyed their parents warily. 'Is there something the matter?' asked Gertie.

'Your father's only flipped his lid. Don't worry

about it, Gertie,' said Mrs Stein shortly. 'Put your foot away please, Jim. I'd like to eat my breakfast.'

Mr Stein returned his foot to its slipper with a bad grace. He glared round at his children, as if daring them to doubt him. 'I saw a ghost last night,' he said, and he sat back to watch his words take effect. This took several moments, during which a small fly almost met a soggy end inside one of the two gaping mouths at the breakfast table. Finally, the penny dropped.

Gertie closed her mouth and immediately opened it again. 'But Dad, you always said only blockheads and nitwits believe in ghosts . . .' she began.

'Blockheaded nitwit? Yes, I think that would be a fair description,' her mother observed acidly, and poured herself another cup of tea.

A second penny dropped.

A cold one, straight down the back of Joe's T-shirt. He squirmed uncomfortably in his seat. 'Oh I don't know,' he muttered. 'If Dad saw something strange in the night, like maybe someone without a head perhaps,' he looked at Gertie, 'then it must have been a ghost, mustn't it? Stands to reason. Couldn't have been anything else.'

'My point exactly, Joe.' Mr Stein thumped the table. 'A headless ghost. How did you know? Did you see it?'

'Well, maybe,' said Joe cautiously.

'That does it!' Mr Stein exploded. 'You can sit there calmly drinking tea, Jill.' He glared at his wife. 'But I for one will not stand by while some headless horror terrorizes my family.' And before anyone could stop him he had darted from the room. 'I'm phoning for an exorcist right now,' he called from the hall.

Joe stared at his mother and Mrs Stein stared at her husband's empty seat. But Gertie had other things on her mind. She helped herself to cereal and tried not to look too pointedly at the full washing-machine, which was right in her mother's line of vision. Any minute now Mrs Stein would notice it and that, thought Gertie, would be it. Full stop, end of story. She ran through all the distraction tactics she knew. There was always the milk. She could spill that, but it occurred to her that this course of action might lead her mother directly to the washing-machine. Instead, she coughed loudly, caught her mother's eye, and: 'Mum, what's an exorcist?' she asked conversationally.

Her mother put down her cup of tea and sighed. 'Someone we don't approve of, Gertie,' she said. 'Someone who goes around pretending to get rid of the ghosts, spirits, poltergeists and whatever else it is that we don't believe in.' Mrs Stein got to her feet. 'Pick up that phone, Jim, and you're history!' she shouted. 'I'm not having one of those charlatans in my house.' And she followed her husband into the hall.

Joe stared at the two empty chairs. He was having difficulty keeping up with events this morning. Perhaps some food would help. He shook himself and reached for the cereal packet.

'Quick,' spluttered Gertie, through her cornflakes. 'We've got to hide Franklin's clothes before Mum spots them.' She dived for the washing-machine.

The cereal packet hovered in mid-air as Joe watched his sister click open the washing-machine and pull out Franklin's suit. His empty bowl waited hopefully, but in vain. Joe blinked and temporarily forgot about his stomach. He put the cereal packet down carefully on the table.

'It's pink,' he breathed.

Sure enough the suit and both Gertie's socks were undeniably, some might say shockingly, pink.

'It must have been the red ink,' said Gertie, bundling the suit up in a plastic bag. 'I told you it wouldn't wash out.'

'You never said it was going to wash in,' her brother retorted. He picked up the cereal packet again and prepared, finally, to pour some into his bowl. Through narrowed eyes, Gertie watched him help himself to milk and sugar, but just as he reached for his spoon her patience snapped.

'Come on, Joe. We haven't got time for all that.' She grabbed him by the elbow and propelled him, protesting, across the room.

'But I haven't had my breakfast yet!'

'Too late. You missed your chance,' she hissed and opened the door.

In the hall Mr Stein was on the telephone. 'Is that the Spiritualist Society?' he inquired. 'Yes, it's urgent . . . Yes, in the middle of the night. It attacked me . . . Yes, yes. You'll send someone as soon as possible? Thanks. I can't tell you how relieved my wife and I will be.' Mr Stein gave the telephone a grateful squeeze.

'Let me just give you our address.'

'I'll kill him,' remarked Mrs Stein to her two children, as they crept past her on the stairs.

10.45 A.M. SATURDAY

Franklin took to dressing up as only a shop dummy can. He enjoyed being a clothes hanger – holding out his arms, lifting his chin, standing still while they fiddled with buttons and adjusted his collar. He was entranced by his gaudy new outfit. And the suit suited him. There was no doubt about it, although Joe had some reservations about Gertie's little extras.

'I'm really not sure about the neckerchief,' he remarked, casting a critical eye over their proud, pink friend. 'If you look closely you can see it's made out of a pair of socks.'

'But he has to have something round his neck to cover the join,' Gertie retorted.

Joe sighed and tried to forget that he had missed his breakfast. From among the rubble that was their den, he managed to unearth Franklin's grey tie. 'This will make him look a bit more ordinary,' he said, knotting it with a flourish. He stood back to admire his handiwork.

'Give us a twirl, Franklin,' he said, and Franklin lurched obligingly round the room.

'There, he looks just great. We could take him out and no one would be any the wiser,' said Gertie. She snatched Franklin's hand and waltzed across the rubble with him.

'What do you think, Franklin?' she asked. Franklin skidded on a marble and fell on his face. 'Think nice pink, Jogert,' he burbled into the floor.

Joe helped him up and brushed him down. 'Poor old Franklin,' he said. 'You can't take two steps in here without tripping over something. We'll have to go out.'

Downstairs, in the kitchen, Mrs Stein was of the same opinion. 'But Jim, we have to go out. There are things to do. Let's forget about ghosts and do the groceries,' she wheedled, dangling a lengthy shopping list under her husband's nose.

But Mr Stein wasn't to be tempted, not by the prospect of tea and cakes in the café afterwards. No, not even by the promise of a new toothbrush and a bottle of whisky. He was immovable.

'I'm immovable,' he informed his wife and folded his arms. 'I'm waiting here for the man from the Spiritualist Society. And that's all there is to it.'

So when Mrs Stein drove off in the car ten minutes later, she went alone.

'Look,' cried Gertie, hanging out of the turret window, 'there's Mum and Dad off to do the shopping. We can sneak Franklin outside for a walk!'

As Gertie later pointed out, a good deal of trouble might have been avoided if only Joe hadn't insisted on raiding the kitchen. Having pondered the unfairness of this for some time, Joe retorted that it was Gertie's fault he was so hungry in the first place. If it came to that, who was the one that said Mum and Dad were out? And anyway, he didn't see why he should take the blame, when she had raced him downstairs – she was as eager as he was for a good scoff.

Whatever the rights and wrongs of it, within seconds of Mrs Stein's departure, Joe, Gertie and Franklin descended on the kitchen like a flock of vultures.

11.15 A.M. SATURDAY

It would be hard to say who was the most taken aback: Gertie and Joe at the spectacle of their father with one foot on the floor and the other jammed under the lens of a high-powered portable microscope, or Mr Stein, finding himself thus discovered.

Having no experience of normal human behaviour, Franklin failed to recognize its absence in the scene before him. He flashed Mr Stein a relaxed and friendly smile.

'Er . . . hello,' said Mr Stein, trying without success to detach his big toe from the microscope. 'Just checking my bruises,' he explained, for the benefit of the tall stranger with the foolish grin.

Mr Stein hoped the man wasn't laughing at him. He had a nice enough face. Good-looking almost, what you might call a model type. But that pink suit was rather outrageous and as for the bare feet, surely people gave up that sort of thing decades ago? By this time Mr Stein had quite forgotten his own embarrassment. He was gaping at Franklin's wheel. OK, it was clean enough, and clearly came off an expensive car, but what sort of person walks about with a wheel under his arm and what was he doing with the kids?

Mr Stein wrenched his foot free, stuffed it firmly into his slipper and stepped forward. 'I don't believe I've had the pleasure . . .' he said.

Roughly translated this means: 'Introduce yourself, turnip-brain.' But how was Franklin to know? If his language skills were skimpy, his social skills were non-existent. He sucked in his cheeks and considered. Gertie and Joe hadn't prepared him for this situation. Let's face it, Gertie and Joe hadn't prepared *themselves* for this situation. They'd only come for a jam sandwich.

Now they were going to have to do the introductions.

They hung their heads. They shuffled their feet. They shrugged their shoulders. They hummed. They hawed. Until at last Gertie spoke up. 'It's Mr Perk . . .' she yelped, as Joe had a brainwave and trod on her toe.

'It's the man from the Spiritualist Society, Dad,' he announced.

Of course, the exorcist! Well, that explained it. You couldn't expect an exorcist to dress like other people. The wheel was probably part of his ghost-busting equipment. 'Well, I summoned the poor man out here,' thought Mr Stein. 'I mustn't be unfriendly.'

He held out his hand. 'Hello, my name's Stein. Pleased to meet you, Mr . . . ?'

Franklin was giving this his full concentration. 'Hello. My name's Stein,' he echoed politely. 'Pleased to meet you, Mr . . . ?'

'Stein!' exclaimed Gertie. 'Mr Franklin Stein, the exorcist, meet Mr Jim Stein, our dad.' She giggled nervously. 'Bit of a coincidence about the surnames, isn't it?' she added. And heaved her toe out from underneath Joe's heel.

'Pleased to meet you, Mr Stein,' repeated Mr Stein, somewhat too heartily. His arm was beginning to ache.

'Pleased to meet you, Mr Stein,' returned the echo, somewhat distractedly. His friends were looking at him in that way they had. He wondered what was going to come next.

What came next was a lot of prodding and nodding and prising of the wheel out from under Franklin's arm. Finally Franklin too held out his hand, a little reluctantly, in case Mr Stein should pull it off.

They shook. Nothing happened.

Franklin put his hand back in his pocket for safe keeping and beamed round good-naturedly. There was a long, uncomfortable silence, during which Mr Stein wondered what he'd got himself involved in. Maybe he'd rather just put up with the ghost.

'Can I show you where it happened?' he asked at last. He gave the visitor a curious look. 'Would you care to leave your wheel here, or do you need it for the exorcism?'

'Exorcism,' repeated the pink fellow. He smiled. 'Yes, wheel,' he observed and patted the thing proudly.

Mr Stein led the way upstairs. He was feeling rather out of his depth. 'Bit of an eccentric, this pink chap,' he thought, 'and rather unnerving the way he repeats your own words back at you.'

He looked over his shoulder at his visitor, who was now following him meekly along the corridor. 'Not exactly worldly-wise,' thought Mr Stein. 'but very pleasant and the children seem to like him.' They were sticking to the exorcist like glue. Aloud he said, 'It was just here.' He stopped outside the bedroom door.

'Door,' intoned Franklin. He pressed his hands against its wooden surface.

'Door,' he repeated. He wasn't quite sure what was expected of him, but at least they'd all know he could recognize a door when he saw one, even if it didn't look much like the picture in *Baby's First Alphabet*.

'Perhaps I should open it and then it will be ajar,' quipped Mr Stein. He was beginning to wish he had listened to his wife. The whole situation was really very awkward. But it was too late to back out now. He stepped forward and opened the door.

Franklin stared in disbelief. He knew what a jar was. It was in the book, and this certainly wasn't one. 'Jar, Jogert?' he inquired and shook his head gravely. His neck started to click, but it seemed as if once he'd started he couldn't stop.

Mr Stein gripped Joe's arm. Things were hotting up. 'He's going into a trance,' he whispered. 'They do, you know.' He felt a thrill of excitement and, 'Stand back, children,' he shouted, as Franklin shook his head so violently that it spun right round on his shoulders.

Mr Stein had never seen anything like it in his life before. If only he had his notebook with him, a camera, a microscope, anything! What a turn-up for the science books. He stared wide-eyed at his visitor, who blinked once or twice, made a strange croaking sound, then spun his head right round the other way. He looked like someone who was having a particularly bumpy ride on a roller-coaster. He had even closed his eyes.

'This is amazing,' gabbled Mr Stein, rubbing his hands with glee. 'I've heard these things happen but I never believed it before. What a shame Mum isn't here to see it. You kids will tell her, won't you?'

His children ignored him. They watched in horrified silence as their friend spun his head clockwise twice, then anti-clockwise three times.

'Any minute now his head's going to come off and then Dad really will flip,' thought Joe. He stared at his sister. 'Stop him,' he mouthed and Gertie swung into action.

'Mr Stein,' she called, tugging one of the pink sleeves urgently, 'Franklin!' The head jolted to a halt and the eyes popped open. They gazed round blankly for a moment, realized they were facing the wrong direction and rolled upwards to watch the ceiling while the head swivelled into its correct position. There was a loud click as something slipped into place.

'Oh, Gertie, why did you stop him?' cried Mr Stein in irritation. 'It was just getting interesting.' He turned to the visitor. 'How are you feeling?' he asked, remembering his manners.

Franklin rubbed his neck. 'No head near,' he explained.

'That's my ghost!' cried Mr Stein. 'It had no head. It's near by you say? Have you got rid of it?'

'OK now. No more no head,' said Franklin emphatically, and he patted his neck to show that his head was still firmly attached to his shoulders and that's where it was going to stay.

Mr Stein thought he meant the ghost. 'No

more? You mean you've done it, you've got rid of him?' he demanded.

'No more no head,' Franklin reassured him.

'Well, that is a relief,' said Mr Stein. But he felt unaccountably disappointed. If only Gertie hadn't interrupted the fellow. It had all been so very interesting. A real eye-opener. Mr Stein felt as if he had stumbled upon something that rewrote the laws of science. He was not about to let it slip through his fingers.

He hung around in the corridor for a while, making small talk, but really the exorcist was so difficult to understand it was like talking to a crossword puzzle. And Joe and Gertie were clearly uncomfortable. It must have been a bit of a shock for them, he supposed, when the man's head whizzed round like a Catherine-wheel. Not really the sort of thing kids should be subjected to. Reluctantly he led the way downstairs.

He came to a standstill in the hall and played for time. He couldn't possibly let the chap leave yet. There were too many unanswered questions. What did the wheel have to do with it all? And what was that stuff earlier on about a jar of yogurt? Just then the front door burst open and in staggered a mountain of shopping. Mr Stein hurried forward to greet it.

'Oh, darling, that was quick! Here, let me help

you.' He relieved his wife of several carrier bags. 'This is Mr Franklin Stein, the exorcist,' he said.

Mrs Stein barely glanced at the man. 'Pleased to meet you, I'm sure,' she said, in a voice that clearly indicated the opposite, and she marched into the kitchen. Her husband bustled after her.

'Bit of a weirdo,' he whispered, rolling his eyes towards the door.

'A blockheaded nitwit you mean?' inquired Mrs Stein icily.

'I suppose so. Doesn't speak much, but ever so pleasant. I've just invited him to lunch.'

1.00 P.M. SATURDAY

Meals, in the Stein household, were usually relaxed occasions, when Mrs and Mr Stein would discuss their work and leave Joe and Gertie to flick peas at one another in peace.

Not any more. And if today's breakfast was anything to go by, lunch was likely to be brief and bloody.

At one end of the table sat Mr Stein, consumed with curiosity about his guest. Mrs Stein sat opposite, also consumed with emotion, in this case rage. Trapped between their parents and biting their nails with anxiety were Gertie and Joe.

As for their guest, he settled back in the chair next to Gertie and mulled over his instructions. 'Do exactly what everyone else does, and we might just get through this in one piece,' Jogert had said. When you only know a few dozen naming words and haven't yet moved on to the doing words, this isn't such an easy idea to grasp, so Gertie and Joe had been forced to perform a hasty mime to illustrate what copying was.

They were developing something of a talent for

acting. For once, Franklin knew exactly what was expected of him. With a confident smile and an expert flourish of the serving spoons, he now followed Gertie's example and attacked the salad bowl.

Mrs Stein regarded the lettuce leaf on her guest's plate. 'I'm afraid most of the salad unaccountably vanished in the middle of the night,' she remarked. 'No doubt, down the throat of a ravenous ghost.'

Her irony was lost on her husband. 'Talk sense, Jill. How could it eat if it didn't have a head?' said Mr Stein. 'Anyway, the ghost's gone,' he added, 'thanks to our friend here.' And he made a sudden jerking motion with his head.

His wife's jaw dropped. 'Great. Now he's developing a nervous twitch,' she thought.

Aloud she said: 'Well, thank goodness for that. Perhaps we won't have to talk about it any more.' And she threw the exorcist a forbidding look. He was, she noticed, having some difficulty with the 'everyone for themselves, grab the grub and guzzle' serving methods favoured in the Stein household. 'Here, let me help you with that,' she said, whisking his plate aloft and piling it high.

She dumped the plate back down in front of the exorcist, who gazed solemnly round the table and picked up his fork.

No, he wasn't quite the smarmy confidence

trickster she had expected. In fact, with his short hair style, extraordinarily white teeth and uncertain manner, he was much more of a boy-next-door type, thought Mrs Stein. Of course the bare feet were a little odd – she had noticed them straight away. And the suit was very unusual, not just the colour but the style. She had seen one like that very recently, only grey not pink. Now where was it? Of course, the strange man who had tried to eat her car! She shot the exorcist a piercing glance. No, this guy had a lot more hair, and teeth too. Those suits must be coming back into fashion, she decided.

'I like your suit,' she said suddenly.

The sole of Gertie's heavy-duty boot descended on Franklin's unprotected foot and he realized that his big moment had arrived. He paused, remembering Jogert's instructions, and decided to plump for something Mrs Stein had said earlier. 'Thank . . .' he began but, before he could press on with the sentence, Mrs Stein leant forward.

'You know, of course,' she confided, 'that I think this exorcism thing is a lot of mumbo jumbo.'

This time Franklin wasn't having any interruptions. 'Thank goodness for that.' He trotted the words out smartly. 'Perhaps we won't have to talk about it any more.'

Mrs Stein chuckled. 'You took the words out of my mouth!' she said.

Her daughter choked and had to be thumped on the back.

Her guest beamed. See, anyone could get the hang of this conversation thing. It was easy. He looked round the table once more and set to work with his fork.

What an agreeable man, thought Mrs Stein. No airs about him at all and it didn't look as if he was going to bore them with tales of the supernatural. She smiled and caught her husband's eye. There he went, jerking his head again! If only he'd stop. It really was most disconcerting.

Joe, meanwhile, toyed with his food. He was ravenous, but all this nervous tension was doing funny things to his insides. He jabbed a piece of tomato and raised it slowly to his mouth. His stomach winced. 'How can you eat at a time like this?' it griped. 'Easy, I swallow and leave the rest to you,' Joe told it grimly. He glanced across at Franklin and the tomato lodged itself somewhere just past his tonsils. How could they have forgotten! The dummy didn't know how to eat!

Franklin was taking great pains to obey orders. He was copying Gertie, shovelling forkfuls of pie and lettuce into his mouth. Like Gertie, he chewed. And, unlike Gertie, chewed and chewed, sixty, seventy, a hundred times. But the food didn't seem to go away.

It was not, Joe thought, the most attractive sight he had ever seen.

Joe swallowed noisily, hoping Franklin would take the hint.

'Joseph!' exclaimed Mrs Stein, and suddenly noticed that her husband was pointing at his forehead and making a spinning motion with his finger.

Really, this was too much! The children ate like pigs and their father made rude gestures at the dinner table. What *would* their guest think? She closed her eyes.

Mr Stein sighed and gave up the hand signals. Jill probably wouldn't believe the exorcist's head had spun right round, anyway. He turned to Franklin. If only the man would stop chewing for a moment, maybe he could ask him a question. At last he could contain himself no longer.

'Er, Franklin – may I call you Franklin?' he began. 'I'd be very interested to learn what you use *that* for,' and he pointed to the wheel, which was propped against the leg of Franklin's chair.

Fortunately Mr and Mrs Stein were spared the sight of Franklin spilling the contents of his mouth back on to his dinner plate, for at that moment the doorbell rang and they both got up to answer it.

'Wheel,' mumbled Franklin and watched with interest as Joe whipped away his plate, emptied it into the bin and replaced it.

'Thank goodness for that,' he said. 'Perhaps we won't . . .'

'Shhh!' ordered Joe.

And then they heard the voice, smooth and unwelcome as an oil slick.

'Susie from the Spiritualist Society gave me a call,' it said, and the hairs stood up on the back of Gertie's neck. She gripped her knife and fork for support.

'Of course, I would have come earlier,' the voice continued, louder now, as its owner brought it with him into the room. 'But I'm afraid some yob vandalized my car and it was at the garage all morning.'

At this point Joe fainted into his dinner. 'Perk!' yelped Franklin, subsiding into a squeak for reasons mainly to do with his foot and Gertie's boot. His face, as he obediently lowered it to rest in his plate, wore an expression of resignation. Gertie gaped. That's not what she had meant at all. And now she was left sticking out like a sore thumb between a couple of ostriches. She took a deep breath and fell forward into her lunch.

'So where's your ghost?' the voice inquired.

Mr Stein cleared his throat. Might as well get any unpleasantness over with as soon as possible. 'I'm afraid there must have been a mix up, Mr Perkins,' he said. 'The exorcism's already been performed.'

'How provoking,' drawled Mr Perkins. 'Of course I shall have to charge a call-out fee, you understand.' He sighed and looked round the room. Rusty washing-machine, grotty-looking cooker, a couple of brats sleeping at the dinner table (what next!) and a fellow with his back to him wearing a pink suit. His gaze came to rest on a large, shiny and familiar-looking wheel.

He glanced quickly back at the children.

'Well, well, well, this is a coincidence,' he remarked, stepping over the table. 'Who says the stars in their travels don't guide our footsteps?' Then he made his first big mistake. He sat down in Mrs Stein's chair.

Prodding Gertie on the shoulder was another mistake. But Perkins wasn't to know that. He just wanted to make sure the brat was paying attention.

'If you'd oblige me by taking your head out of your lunch,' he said. 'I believe we still have a little matter of £400 damages and a stolen wheel to discuss.'

Gertie brushed the pastry from her eyes and stared blankly at the supermarket manager. She wondered why he wasn't wearing his badge today. She wondered when she was going to come up with a fiendish stratagem to see him off once and for all. She wondered where the unpleasant strangling sound was coming from. Finally, she snapped her mouth shut and the noise stopped. Perkins sighed: no point wasting time on a tongue-tied kid. She probably didn't even have a bank account. He turned to the man of the house.

'Perhaps I should explain, Mr Stein,' he said. 'Exorcism is something of a hobby with me. Normally I manage Price's Supermarket in town, which is where I met your children.' He paused and arranged his features into an injured expression, so that Mr Stein would know he was speaking more in sorrow than in anger.

'Not content with allowing their uncle to destroy my shop,' he continued, 'your children then went outside and removed the wheel from my car.'

'Uncle?' Both parents looked bewildered.

'But we haven't any uncles in our family,' said Mr Stein.

There was an uncomfortable silence, during which Joe discovered that some invisible force, possibly his own terror, had plucked him from his seat and propelled him across the room. This left Franklin stranded with his head on his plate, copying nobody at all. Perkins closed in on him at once.

'And who have we here?' observed the supermarket manager, dropping his hard-done-by act and preparing to pounce.

Franklin whipped his hands behind his back

and sat up. 'Keep your head on,' he said, remembering Jogert's well-worn advice.

Mr Stein decided to intervene before the exorcists came to blows. He stepped forward and laid a restraining hand on Perkins's shoulder. 'This is Mr Franklin Stein, who so kindly performed the exorcism for us,' he explained.

'Exorcism? This idiot?' Perkins was outraged. 'I hardly think we would allow blockheads like that in the Spiritualist Society,' he spluttered.

'Oh wouldn't you?' asked Mrs Stein with icy politeness. 'I would have thought it was a necessary qualification for entry.'

Perkins was beginning to get seriously rattled, which is possibly why he made his final, fatal mistake. He held up his hand and waved the woman away. 'Please, Mrs Stein,' he drawled. 'I think this is a matter for your husband and myself, don't you?'

'No, I don't,' objected Mrs Stein. She didn't like this man; she didn't like him sitting in her seat without asking; she didn't like him taking that slimy tone with her daughter; and she certainly didn't like him telling her to shut up.

Well, she wasn't going to shut up. She was going to give him a piece of her mind.

'First of all, Mr Perkins,' she began, and smiled grimly, 'if you want to come into my house and intimidate my guests and frighten my children,

I'm afraid you're going to have to deal with me. Secondly, I may not be able to tell a ghost from a gumtree but I can recognize an out and out charlatan and a bully to boot. Thirdly . . .' but Mrs Stein's third point never made it past her lips because just then there was a discreet tap and Daisy Roberts popped her head round the kitchen door.

1.20 P.M. SATURDAY

'Good afternoon, Jill,' she said brightly. 'Good afternoon Jim. I hope I'm not interrupting anything.'

Daisy was wearing her glasses today, so the briefest of glances told her all she needed to know. There was Joseph, bent double over the washing-machine, and Gertrude, pale and tense beside the fridge. There were the parents, hot, bothered and both looking as if they'd just swallowed something extremely unpleasant. And there, noted Daisy, was the half-eaten meal on the table. She drew her own conclusions.

Her neighbours displayed all the symptoms of food poisoning. Daisy moved cautiously into the middle of the room and hoped no one was about to be sick. 'I'm not interrupting anything?' she repeated.

Mr Stein mopped his brow. 'No, Daisy,' he sighed. 'Do come in. The more the merrier.'

But neither of the Steins' other guests was looking particularly merry, thought Daisy. Try as he might to hide it, something had disagreed badly with the smooth one in the expensive footwear. As for the other gentleman – if you're going to wear a flashy pink suit, you might at least take the trouble to iron it, she commented inwardly. And what were the Steins doing with a car wheel in their kitchen?

The events of the previous night, which she had hurried over to relate, suddenly seemed less pressing to Daisy Roberts. Besides, she didn't relish telling tales on the children in front of complete strangers.

Who on earth were they?

'Hello, I'm Miss Roberts,' she began and glanced meaningfully at Jill, who remembered her manners with a start.

'Daisy, meet Franklin, a family friend,' said Mrs Stein, indicating the flashy pink one. She hesitated, then gestured towards the smooth-looking one. 'And Anthony Perkins,' she added as if he were an afterthought – an unpleasant one at that.

Well, this put quite a different complexion on things. '*The* Anthony Perkins, from the supermarket?' inquired Daisy coldly, and withdrew her hand. Let's see what the drunkard had to say for himself.

But there was nothing apologetic about Mr Perkins. He didn't even bother to look up, just sat there staring at his hands and flexing his fingers. Feeling the effects of last night's over-indulgence no doubt.

'Yes, Price's Supermarket,' he observed at last. 'A managerial position. A respectable position. A position, I might add, of some authority in this town.'

'Oh,' said Daisy, somewhat taken aback by his hostile tone. You'd almost think *he* was the one who'd had his pansies irrecoverably crushed.

'I gave you the chance to avoid unpleasantness,' continued the supermarket manager, in a voice that suggested it was he who had spent all morning trying, in vain, to revive his snapdragons.

'I was quite prepared to accept a token sum in compensation,' he said, 'and what did you do?'

Daisy gasped. The nerve of the man! She hadn't done anything – yet. 'Just you wait, you scoundrel,' she thought.

'I'll tell you what you did, *Mrs Stein*,' snarled Mr Perkins. 'You insulted me!' He paused, then softly added, 'I think it's about time we called the police, don't you?'

What with lack of sleep and all that bother with the flowers this morning, Daisy had had enough. If her late-night intruder wanted to call the police, she was right behind him.

'Yes, Mr Perkins, I rather think we should,' she said.

Now it was Perkins's turn to be taken aback. He hadn't expected anyone to agree with him. In fact, he didn't *want* anyone to agree with him. He just wanted to frighten these people into handing over a large amount of money.

'Excuse me, madam, I don't believe we've met before,' he drawled.

'Oh, but we have, Mr Perkins,' said Daisy. 'We met last night, though possibly you weren't in a fit state to remember.'

Perkins stared at her blankly. No, he couldn't remember. He shook himself and turned to Mr Stein. 'Let me put it to you man to man,' he said. 'Either you hand over a cheque for a thousand pounds, or I call the police.'

Several pairs of eyebrows leapt ceilingwards.

Even Perkins was surprised at himself.

He hadn't intended to state the options quite so bluntly, nor to pitch his 'token sum' quite so high. And he didn't like the way that the long arm of the law kept intruding in his conversation.

'Yes, I think the police will be very interested to hear about your activities, Mr Perkins,' said Daisy sharply. 'I've never seen such appalling behaviour. Trespassing on private property in a state of near undress, trampling the plants, upsetting little children – poor Joseph was quite distraught.'

Not as distraught as Perkins was rapidly becoming. If only this old woman would stop badgering him. 'Really, Madam,' he began. 'I haven't the faintest idea what you're talking about.'

'Don't you Madam me, young man,' snapped Daisy. 'I know your sort. I was going to call the police at the time but, against my better judgement, I let the children talk me out of it. I'll hand it to you, Mr Perkins, you've got a nerve coming up here after your behaviour yesterday.'

'Hand?' asked Perkins nervously. 'Yesterday?'

Surely the old trout didn't know about the horrible incident with the hand?

'I didn't touch his hand!' he gabbled. 'I thought about it afterwards, and I'm sure I didn't. I don't know where all the blood came from, but it was nothing to do with me.'

His eyes darted around the room. He was beginning seriously to dislike this woman with her sensible clothes and genteel hair style. 'How do you know about the hand?' he said slowly – and before Daisy could ask, 'What hand?' he brought his own down hard on the table.

'That's it!' he cried, parting company with what remained of his common sense. There was magic at work here. This awful old woman. That terrible business with the hand. It was the only possible explanation. 'You old witch!' he squawked.

'Well, I never!' spluttered Daisy, stepping rapidly backwards as Perkins shot to his feet.

He was in the grip of righteous and defiant rage. 'You'll never shop in my supermarket again!' he shrieked, directing a shaking finger round the room. 'None of you. Ha! I know how to deal with your sort. I'll hang horseshoes over the door, see if I don't!'

And before they could set upon him with sorcery and foul spells, he snatched up his wheel and ran.

'Get thee behind me Satan!' he screeched from the safety of the doorway. Then stopped transfixed.

'Don't you Madam me young man!' Franklin nodded primly, keeping his eye on the wheel. *He had his head on back to front*.

With a final, blood-curdling scream, the supermarket manager fled.

There was a long, embarrassed silence, before Franklin realized, whoops! he was playing that naughty trick with his head again. He hastily jerked it into a less outrageous position.

'You know, of course, that I think this exorcism stuff is a lot of mumbo jumbo,' he remarked, to anyone who might be listening.

1.28 P.M. SATURDAY

Gertie, Joe, Mrs Stein, Mr Stein and Daisy collapsed around the table in stunned silence. Nobody said a word until, 'Well, I shan't be shopping at Price's again, horseshoes or no horseshoes,' announced Mrs Stein, and the three adults began to speak at once.

Amid the buzz and hubbub, the protestations of a fourth voice passed unnoticed. 'But they always go to bed at nine o'clock,' insisted Franklin. 'Not in your flowerbed, surely?' he gasped and, casting accuracy to the winds, exclaimed with Daisy: 'Witch! And me a bishop's niece . . .'

Unnoticed, that is, except by Gertie and Joe. Their eyes met across the table.

'No more breaking into conversation,' signalled Gertie, raising her right eyebrow.

'No more breaking the laws of physics,' signalled Joe, fluttering his lower left eyelash.

Out of sight under the tablecloth, their fingers snapped round Franklin's wrists like handcuffs.

1.40 P.M. SATURDAY

Daisy got up to go.

'I think it would be best,' she said, sliding her chair under the table and straightening a wrinkle in the cloth, 'if we said nothing more about this unfortunate incident for the moment. I myself will keep an eye out for that Perkins scoundrel.'

'Yes of course, Daisy,' said Mrs Stein. 'And thanks very much for calling in. It's been most instructive.'

Here she frowned at her offspring. They had both finished their meal and were sitting watching the exorcist with their hands in their laps. Hard to believe they tore around the countryside at all hours of the night. But then Mrs Stein didn't know what to believe any more. She certainly hadn't believed her own eyes a few minutes ago when the exorcist's head had turned full circle on his neck.

On her way back from showing Daisy to the door, motherly concern and scientific curiosity had a brief struggle in the breast of Professor Jill Stein. Science won. After all, anyone could see the children were healthy and happy, if sometimes a little overtired. She'd speak to them later. Meanwhile there was the matter of the spinning head to be cleared up. She snatched up a dishtowel and strode over to her husband, who was up to his elbows in the kitchen sink. 'If there's something I don't know about the human skeleton, tell me now,' she hissed, making a great show of drying the cutlery. 'Because according to my information, what your exorcist did with his head is downright impossible.'

'No, not impossible,' whispered Mr Stein. He examined the plate he was washing and allowed himself a smug smile. 'At least, not from a blockhead's point of view.'

His wife sighed. 'O K,' she said. 'You were right and I was wrong.' She glanced across at the table, where Joe, Gertie and the exorcist sat in what she took to be a relaxed and companionable silence. 'I suppose a blockhead would want to take a closer look at this Franklin chap,' she said.

'Naturally,' Mr Stein nudged his wife and raised a finger to his lips.

'But how?' she hissed, clattering the cutlery in its drawer. 'How can we take a closer look at him? We can't exactly ask him to move in here for the advancement of science.'

'Now that,' whispered Mr Stein, shaking the suds off his hands and relieving his wife of the dishtowel, 'is a very good idea.'

He paused a moment to collect his thoughts, then unrolled his sleeves, cleared his throat and strode across to the exorcist.

'Well, Franklin, how about a lift home after all the excitement?' he suggested, clapping his guest on the back. At which point, two pairs of jittery hands accidentally pinched the guest under the table. 'Yowch!' The guest started to his feet. The unseen hands clung on for dear life. The table lurched and the guest bounced back into his chair.

Mr Stein pressed his advantage. 'Where do you live, old boy?' he asked and the unseen hands squeezed Franklin tightly, willing him to concentrate. This must be important. Franklin furrowed his brow and searched for the right word.

'A tip. A dump,' he said. Now what else did they call it? Oh yes. 'I live in Junksville.' And he pulled the sort of face Joe and Gertie wore when they said these things. He was about to elaborate when Mr Stein thumped him again. He had heard enough.

'Well, that settles it!' he cried. 'You must move in with us. Don't you agree, Jill?'

'Of course,' said Mrs Stein, suddenly materializing beside her husband. 'We've a ridiculous amount of space here. One of our turret rooms would suit you nicely, Franklin. The one next to the laboratory would be ideal. We'll run you a cable through for electricity. It's a lovely room, you know, with a great view.'

Franklin blinked. Laboratory? Electricity? Why people couldn't stick to ordinary words like xylophone and zebra, he'd never know. This was terrible. He was expecting the man to hit him again at any moment. He closed his eyes and blindly repeated the first thing that came into his head.

'The one next to the laboratory would be ideal,' said Franklin and Mr Stein whistled, flung his dishtowel in the air and caught it with a flourish.

'Well, that's it then,' he said, thumping the exorcist on the back yet again. 'Joe and Gertie will show you up there. Help yourself to any furniture you fancy out of the west wing and make yourself at home. You're one of the family now.'

With that, the unseen hands released their hold on Franklin, slithered out from under the table and pummelled him on the back.

2.05 P.M. SATURDAY

'Uncle Franklin!' gasped Joe, trying to keep his voice down as they fell up the stairs.

'Uncle Franklin!' cried Gertie as they tore across the lab.

'Not in the flowerbed,' squawked Franklin as they propelled him up the turret stair. 'You're one of the family now!'

Eight hours and two dozen bin-bags later the den was restored, if not to its former glory, at least to a state of order. The west wing had lost a bed, a chest of drawers, several blankets, a pillow and a rather nice pair of curtains, which now hung in the turret window, framing a crescent moon and a dusky sky.

Tea had been eaten (by those who ate tea). Gertie and Joe had been whisked away to wherever it was they went at this time of day and Franklin was alone – alone with his new bed.

First he tested the mattress. Then he buried his face in the pillows. Finally he slipped between the sheets. 'And me a bishop's niece,' he sighed. Ah, the bliss of being tucked up in bed with a torch and a good book. The short-lived bliss.

9.26 P.M. SATURDAY

Bristling with torches, jumpers askew over pyjamas, in burst Gertie and Joe.

'Bed, Jogert,' said Franklin, by way of a greeting. He patted his pillow and pointed to the picture on page two of his book. 'Jogert bed?' he queried and yawned widely.

But they weren't taking the hint. They threw themselves down on his feet and squirmed about in that purposeless way people do after too much excitement and not enough sleep.

Gertie had a telescope which she trained on various objects around the room. Joe rummaged through his knapsack. They were both looking for something to do.

'Where shall we go tonight?' Gertie asked.

Joe grunted and tipped the contents of his knapsack on the floor.

There was a long silence, at the end of which Joe found what he was looking for on his wrist.

9.30 P.M. SATURDAY

'Do you realize it's exactly forty-eight hours since we first found Franklin?' said Joe.

'No, I didn't,' said Gertie, stifling a yawn. 'That means we've only known him two days. Amazing really. It seems like a lifetime.'

'Are you tired?' she added suddenly, directing the telescope at her brother's nose.

Joe rubbed his face. 'Not very,' he said. 'Why? Are you?'

'Not very,' said Gertie guardedly. She pointed her telescope at Franklin's book and slowly brought the rosy red apple on its cover into focus.

'I know,' she said and twirled the telescope like a baton. 'Let's go and raid Daisy's apple tree. Franklin will love that.'

'OK,' Joe said. He swung his legs off the bed and stretched hugely. 'Come on, Franklin. Stir your stumps.'

But Franklin never answered. Behind the apple-decked covers of his favourite book, somewhere between the umbrella and the violin, he had fallen fast asleep.